~FIRST GREEK MYTHS~

KING MIDAS'S GOLDFINGERS

For Jake and Fleur Pirotta
S.P.

To my boys
J.L.

Series reading consultant: Prue Goodwin, a lecturer in
Literacy in Education at the University of Reading

ORCHARD BOOKS
96 Leonard Street, London EC2A 4XD
Orchard Books Australia
32/45-51 Huntley Street, Alexandria, NSW 2015
This text was first published in Great Britain
in the form of a gift collection called *First Greek Myths*, in 2003
This edition first published in hardback in Great Britain in 2005
First published in paperback in 2006
Text © Saviour Pirotta 2005
Cover illustrations © Jan Lewis 2003
Inside illustration © Jan Lewis 2005
The rights of Saviour Pirotta to be identified as the author and
Jan Lewis to be identified as the illustrator of this work
have been asserted by them in accordance with the
Copyright, Designs and Patents Act, 1988.
A CIP catalogue record for this book is available from the British Library.
ISBN 978 1 84362 782 1
5 7 9 10 8 6 4
Printed in China
Orchard Books is a division of Hachette Children's Books,
an Hachette UK company.
www.hachette.co.uk

~FIRST GREEK MYTHS~
KING MIDAS'S GOLDFINGERS

BY SAVIOUR PIROTTA
ILLUSTRATED BY JAN LEWIS

ORCHARD BOOKS

~ CAST LIST ~

KING MIDAS
(King My-das)

A rich king

THE SATYR
(the sat-ear)

A magical creature –
half man and half goat

Gold, gold, shimmering, glimmering gold. Every night King Midas went to bed thinking about his gold.

He had lots of it, all locked away in secret places so no one else could touch it.

The king's daughter was glad her father had so much gold. She just wished that he didn't have to count it every day. Then, perhaps, he could spend some time with her.

One day, the little princess
disturbed King Midas in the
middle of counting his treasure.

"Father," she cried, "come
and play in the garden with me."

7

"I'm sorry, my little princess," said the king. "Not just now. I must finish counting my gold. One golden goblet, two golden cups..."

You see, King Midas was
very greedy. He wanted to have
more gold than any other king
in the world!

When at last all his gold had been counted and safely hidden away again, the king headed for the garden to find his daughter.

He was still thinking of how to get more gold, when he saw a satyr, an odd looking creature who was half man and half goat.

"Can I pick an orange from your tree?" asked the satyr. "Of course," answered King Midas, still thinking about his gold.

The satyr took some fruit.

"You deserve a reward for your
kindness," the satyr said. "Tell me
what you wish for most in the
world, and I'll grant it to you."

"What do I wish for most in the world?" thought King Midas. There were lots of things he could ask for. A pony for his little princess...

or a good harvest for his farmers.

But finally he said, "I want
everything I touch to turn to gold!"

"Are you sure?" asked the satyr.

"Yes! Yes! Yes!" Midas assured him. "At last I'll have more gold than any other king!"

"Very well," said the satyr as he trotted off. "Your wish is granted."

King Midas looked at the trees and flowers around him. "Can I really change everything to gold just by touching it?" he wondered.

He picked a flower and...yes!...
it turned to solid gold.

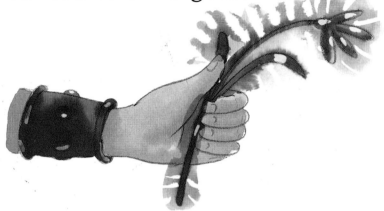

He tapped a snail on its shell
and that, too, turned to gold!

The king ran indoors. He
touched bowls and basins...

He ran his fingers along
curtains... Everything turned
to gold.

King Midas called his servants.
"Bring me wine. I want to celebrate!"

Quickly, the servants poured
the king some wine. King Midas
held it to his lips but…the wine
turned to solid gold the moment
it touched him.

"Meat!" he roared. A servant handed him a platter of partridges cooked in honey but...more gold!

"What have I done?" King Midas sighed. "I'll never be able to eat or drink again. I'll starve."

Just then his little princess came running in. She was about to give her father a big hug, when…

"STOP! Don't touch me," King Midas shouted.

The princess looked sad. "Papa, why not? What have I done?"

"Oh, my little princess. You haven't done anything," cried the king. "It's me. I'm cursed. Everything I touch turns to gold."

"But you love gold, father," the little princess said. "Aren't you pleased?"

King Midas sighed. "You can't drink or eat gold, Princess. You can't hug it. What shall I do?"

"Would the person who put the curse on you take it away again?" said the princess.

"That's it!" said King Midas. He ran out of the palace, leaving a trail of golden footprints behind him.

When he caught up with the
satyr, he fell to his knees.

"Please take back your gift,"
he begged.

"Don't you want everything
you touch to turn to gold after
all?" asked the satyr.

"No," said King Midas, his head bowed in shame.

"I think you've learned your lesson," said the satyr. "Go and wash in the river. It will cure you."

The king ran to the river. He took off his clothes and dived in. King Midas scrubbed his hands over and over again. Then he picked up a shell, held it tightly and...it remained an ordinary shell.

The golden touch had flowed
out of him and away on the river.

King Midas dropped the shell
and scooped water to his dry lips.
How good it tasted!

Then he put on his clothes and
hurried back to his palace. There
he gave his little daughter the
biggest hug ever.

"See, my little princess,"
said the king happily. "Some
things are much more precious
than gold!"

~FIRST GREEK MYTHS~

KING MIDAS'S GOLDFINGERS

BY SAVIOUR PIROTTA ⌐ ILLUSTRATED BY JAN LEWIS

And enjoy a little magic with these First Fairy Tales:

Orchard books are available from all good bookshops,
or can be ordered from our website: www.orchardbooks.co.uk,
or telephone 01235 827702, or fax 01235 827703.